Iris is the resident artist of the garden. Although she is very shy and quiet, her deep emotions show on her wonderful canvases.

Pitterpat is a fluffy and devoted kitten. She and Rose-Petal have an extra-special relationship and are rarely seen apart. Pitterpat has saved Rose-Petal from trouble on more than one occasion.

P.D. Centipede, the athlete of Rose-Petal Place, sees life as one big game. He is full of pep, and can be seen jogging around the garden every morning.

Seymour J. Snailsworth is a snail of great wisdom. He carries his unique and elegant home on his back, and can always be called upon for a word or two of advice.

Tumbles the Hedgehog is a happy-go-lucky fellow who is always full of fun and laughs. The girls love to have Tumbles around, even if he does trip and stumble a lot!

Unfortunately, there is a dark and untended part of the garden where nothing grows. There, in Tin-Can Castle, live *Nastina,* an evil spider, and her hateful assistant, *Horace Fly.* Nastina's goal in life is to get rid of Rose-Petal and make herself Queen of Rose-Petal Place. So we are always on our guard against Nastina and her wicked tricks.

With all of us working and playing together, Rose-Petal Place remains an enchanted garden full of sunshine and flowers, music and laughter. Please come join us!

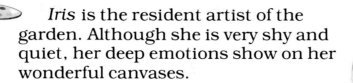

Library of Congress Cataloging in Publication Data: Buss, Nancy. Rose-Petal's Big Decision. Rose-Petal. Rose-Petal Place. SUMMARY: Rose-Petal receives a letter offering her a recording contract, without knowing it is a trick by the evil spider Nastina to get her away from the garden.
[1. Gardens—Fiction. 2. Flowers—Fiction. 3. Spiders—Fiction] I. Title. II. Series.
PZ7.B9656Le 1984 [E] 83-23818 ISBN 0-910313-52-0
Manufactured in the United States of America 1 2 3 4 5 6 7 8 9 0

ROSE-PETAL PLACE™

Rose-Petal's
Big Decision

by Nancy Buss
Pictures by Pat Paris and Sharon Ross-Moore

One fine, sunny day Rose-Petal received a very important letter. She was so excited about it that she could hardly wait to tell her friends. She ran from her house waving the letter in the air, Pitterpat close at her heels.

"Sunny Sunflower . . . Orchid . . . I've been offered a record contract! They want me to sing! Iris, Lily Fair . . . come quickly!"

Sunny Sunflower grabbed the letter as Rose-Petal hugged Iris and danced around and around with her on the garden path.

"What does it say?" asked Daffodil. "Read it to us."

Sunny Sunflower read in a loud, clear voice:

Dear Miss Rose-Petal:

    After hearing you sing last week at
Carnation Hall, we are pleased to invite
you to come to our recording studio and
make a record. Your beautiful voice will
surely help all parts of the garden
become as healthy and as happy as the
area near where you live. We are located
about an eight-hour "roadster" ride
from Rose-Petal Place and you would
have to stay here at least two weeks to
complete the record. We hope you can
join us.

        Sincerely,
        Garden Recording Company

"You've just got to go!" Sunny Sunflower declared. "Call them right now! Tell them you'll come."

"A recording studio! I wonder what you should wear? " asked Orchid.

Lily Fair did a pirouette and then practiced a sweeping bow. "Imagine making a real record . . ." she said dreamily.

"Imagine the money!" Daffodil said, whipping out her calculator. "If they pay you . . . uh . . . for two weeks . . . that's . . ."

Rose-Petal giggled. "Wait. Not so fast. I've got to think."

But before anyone could think, Lily Fair, who was still practicing her sweeping bows and curtsies, lost her balance. She fell into Orchid, who fell into the bed of daisies where Horace Fly had been quietly listening. He quickly flew off but not before giving Orchid a little kiss on the end of her nose.

Orchid screamed, "Get the disgusting creature away from me! I'll simply die if he touches me again!" She flailed her arms and legs around so much that Pitterpat, thinking it was a game, scampered over and swatted her with his tail.

Sunny collapsed in laughter. "Too bad Orchid can't go with you as the Rose-Petal Place clown," she said, wiping tears from her eyes.

"I fail to see anything funny," Orchid fumed.

Rose-Petal hid a smile and gently led Pitterpat away from Orchid. Then she helped Orchid and Lily Fair to their feet.

"Come to my house," she said. "We'll have some lemonade and talk this over."
And that's exactly what they did.

Meanwhile, in another part of the garden, the dark, dreary part, the evil spider Nastina was celebrating the success of her plan by mixing up a special new beauty potion for herself.

"It worked!" she cackled, to Horace Fly, her repulsive assistant. "She believed that phony letter I sent her! I am a genius after all . . . aren't I, Horace?"

"Sure, sure," muttered Horace.

Nastina threw the bottle containing the brown beauty potion straight at Horace Fly. It knocked him off the sardine can that Nastina used for a bed.

Nastina stared at her reflection in her cracked mirror. A drop of the sticky, brown liquid dripped from her nose. "At last I'm getting rid of her," she said. "And with Rose-Petal gone for even a week or two, I can get control of the garden."

"But the others will still be here," Horace Fly said, picking himself up from the floor. He munched on an orange peel he had found there.

"Don't worry about them," Nastina said. She smiled. "I have my plans. *You* may even get to keep the lovely Orchid for your own. But now I must go and congratulate our young singer."

When Nastina arrived at Rose-Petal's, she found her surrounded by all her friends. They were all talking and laughing excitedly.

"We'll see who they come to when you're gone," Nastina thought to herself. Then she smiled as Rose-Petal hurried over to greet her.

"What wonderful news, my dear," Nastina crooned. "I'm so glad you'll be leaving . . . uh . . . I mean I'm so glad you have this marvelous opportunity! I'll be hurt if you don't let me help."

"Why, thank you, Nastina," Rose-Petal said, blushing slightly. "It's very kind of you. In fact, everyone is being so kind . . ." A tear slid down Rose-Petal's cheek. "I'm going to miss you all if I go."

"What do you mean 'if you go'?" Sunny Sunflower said. "Of course you're going. Things here will be just fine."

"Of course they will be," Nastina agreed. "I will personally take charge of the garden while you're getting ready to go. And, of course, while you're away. And a party — I must give you a going-away party! Say that you'll come."

And Rose-Petal promised she would, because she was the kind of girl who would never hurt anyone's feelings.

The next few days were busy ones for the residents of Rose-Petal Place — especially for Nastina.

True to her word, she *did* take charge of the garden.

But Nastina's idea of taking care of the garden was very different from Rose-Petal's. When Rose-Petal tended the garden, her singing made the flowers bloom and the seedlings sprout. Nastina didn't do anything to help the plants. So it was no surprise when they began to wither, droop, and die.

And then there was the party. Nastina spent hours pouring over her books for spells and recipes, and more hours searching for special ingredients. Soon, her rusty Tin-Can Castle reeked with the odors of her cooking. And Horace Fly, always hungry, watched the preparations with great interest.

"Smells like nothing I've ever smelled before," he said, dipping into one of the huge pots. "What is it?"

Nastina knocked the spoon from his hand.

"It's for the party, you stupid thing! It's my special sleeping potion," cackled Nastina.

"We'll see that Orchid gets just enough to put her to sleep for a little while. As for Rose-Petal and the others . . . just leave them to me. I've waited a long time for this." Nastina looked positively happy as she stirred her evil brew.

Meanwhile, Rose-Petal and her friends were busy preparing for Rose-Petal's visit to the recording studio. Orchid helped to choose her clothes, and Sunny Sunflower helped to pack them. Iris and Lily Fair gathered the music that Rose-Petal would perform, and Daffodil saw to the travel arrangements. Everyone was still so excited for Rose-Petal that no one noticed that things were not as they should be in the garden. No one, that is, except Rose-Petal.

She loved Rose-Petal Place more than anyone
and could feel the change in her surroundings.
The flowers that were once so beautiful were
dying. Many of the trees had lost their leaves,
and the birds that had lived in the branches had
left. She found the flagstone paths covered with
webs. There was a flea-market sign outside
Carnation Hall, and everywhere she went she
heard arguing and grumbling over rules Nastina
had made. The garden was no longer a happy
place.

But Rose-Petal did nothing until P. D.
Centipede came to her one day. "Nastina caught
Tumbles the Hedgehog playing in her part of the
garden," he said. "To punish him, she's keeping
him in a cage just outside her castle."

"You must be mistaken," Rose-Petal said
gently.

But she went to see, and sure enough, there was the poor hedgehog, lonely and caged. It was then, as she looked around her, that Rose-Petal made her decision.

The place where Nastina lived had always been swampy, smelly, and filled with rubbish. But now all of Rose-Petal Place was starting to look like the area around Tin-Can Castle. Rose-Petal couldn't let that happen. She couldn't go away knowing that the garden would not be the same when she returned. So, Rose-Petal released Tumbles from his small prison and knocked on Nastina's door.

"I've let Tumbles go free," she said, when Nastina answered the door. "And what's more, the past few days have given me a taste of what life would be like in Rose-Petal Place if I left. I don't like what I've seen at all, so I've decided not to go. Thanks for helping me come to this important decision. I hope you haven't gone to a lot of bother."

Nastina was so angry that she could hardly
answer Rose-Petal.

Finally, she said, clenching her teeth, "Oh, no,
my dear. It's quite all right. No bother at all."

Then Nastina slammed the door and threw her shoes, one after another, after another, after another, at poor Horace.

"That does it!" she cried. "All my perfect plans ruined!"

"I'm sure you'll come up with something else . . ." whimpered Horace Fly, ducking the flying shoes.

Later, Rose-Petal gathered her friends together and told them of her decision.

"There will be other recording contracts," she said. "But right now I'm just not ready to leave this place and all of you — my friends."

Of course all her friends were delighted that Rose-Petal was staying since they loved her very much. And they decided to give a big party in her honor anyway. Instead of a "Going Away" party, they changed it to a "Glad You're Staying" party. Since Nastina wasn't invited, no one got poisoned, and it was the best party anyone could ever remember.

I'm Elmer the elm tree, and I know everything there is to know about this beautiful garden because I keep it all recorded in my diary. Let me introduce you to the delightful group of characters who have made Rose-Petal Place their home.

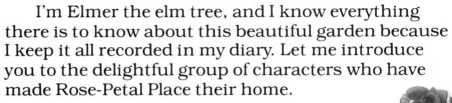

Rose-Petal is the natural leader and protector of Rose-Petal Place. She is as talented as she is beautiful and sweet. Her magical singing keeps the garden blooming, and her good common sense keeps everyone in it safe and happy.

Sunny Sunflower is Rose-Petal's best friend. As is often the case with best friends, they are opposites in many ways. Sunny is a tomboy who always says exactly what's on her mind. You might say she's "spice" to Rose-Petal's "sugar."

Lily Fair is a dreamer whose dearest wish is to be a star. She is sincere and dedicated and can be seen practicing her dancing at all hours of the day and night.

Daffodil is all business. She runs the Bouquet Boutique, where all the girls go for their beautiful clothes. She has big plans for her future as a businesswoman and is never without her flower-shaped calculator.

Orchid is Daffodil's best customer. She loves to pamper herself and spends most of her time on self-improvement. When Orchid is not actually shopping, she is thinking about it!